This
Bear with Sticky Paws
book belongs to:

· · · · · · · · · · · · · · · · · ·

KEEP YOUR PAWS OFF!

for Martha
with love

and for my small friend
Conrad

ORCHARD BOOKS
338 Euston Road, London NW1 3BH
Orchard Books Australia
Level 17/207 Kent Street, Sydney, NSW 2000

First published in 2007 by Orchard Books
First published in paperback in 2008

Text and illustrations © Clara Vulliamy 2007

The right of Clara Vulliamy to be identified as the author
and illustrator of this work has been asserted by her in
accordance with the Copyright, Designs and Patents Act, 1988.

A CIP catalogue record for this book is available from
the British Library.

ISBN 978 1 84616 306 7

1 3 5 7 9 10 8 6 4 2

Printed in China

Orchard Books is a division of Hachette Children's Books,
an Hachette Livre UK company.

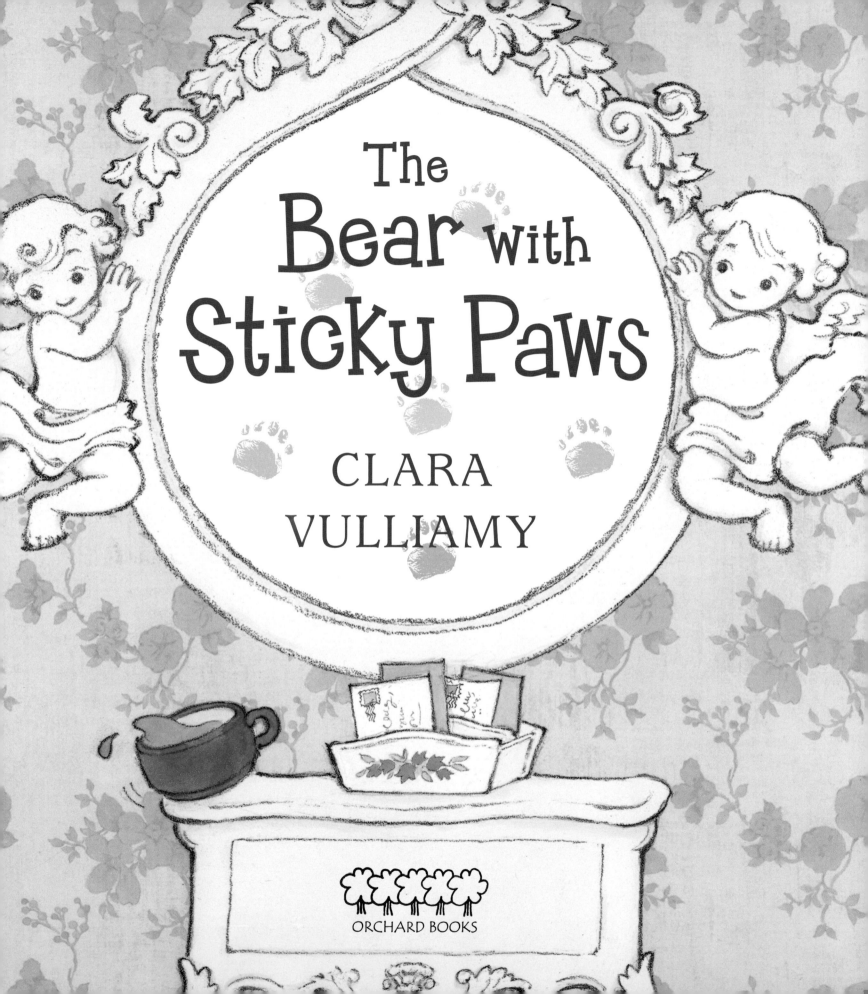

The Bear with Sticky Paws

CLARA VULLIAMY

ORCHARD BOOKS

There's a girl called Pearl
and she's being very grumpy,
stamping her little feet
and slamming the door.
She says,

"I don't want all this **breakfast!**"

and throws down her spoon.

"**NO**, I won't wash my face.
    NO, I won't brush my hair.
NO, I won't get dressed . . ."

"NO! NO!
NO! NO!
NO! NO!
NO! NO!
NO!"

Until Mum calls out,

"*Stop!*"

And –

oh NO!

She's gone!

But then,

bing-
bong!

There's a bear on the doorstep,
a small white tufty one,
standing on his suitcase to reach the bell.

"Breakfast?" says the bear,
sniffing the air.

"BREAKFAST?
Yes, please!"

The bear eats it all.
"MORE!"
says the bear.

Pearl makes

5 pancakes,

8 pieces of jammy toast

and 9 bowls of porridge.

And – oh NO!

Sticky paws everywhere!

But the bear
doesn't care . . .
"Let's PLAY!"
says the bear.

He's
snuffling
and sniffling . . .

. . . hiding
and sliding . . .

leaping
and climbing!

And –
oh NO!

He's on top of the wardrobe!

"Lunch time!" calls Pearl.
"UP HERE!" says the bear.
So Pearl has to throw the food up to him –

7 pieces of pizza,

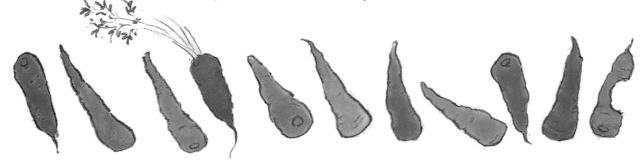

11 carrots

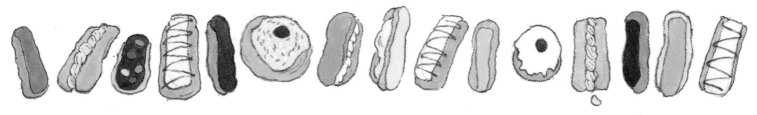

and 15 sugar buns.

"Let's do dressing up!" says the bear.
"OK," says Pearl.
And – oh NO!

Down comes the curtain.

But then,
"SPARKLE!"
says the bear.
And – oh NO!
It's Mum's stuff,
too.

"Better go in the garden," says Pearl.

 "SWIM!" says the bear.

And –

 oh NO!

He jumps right in the fountain.

Pearl fetches tea. There are

9 honey sandwiches,

11 bowls of milk

and too many ice creams to count.

"I'm tired," says Pearl.

"NOT TIRED!" says the bear.

"Come on," says Pearl,
taking him by a sticky paw.
"It's your bedtime."

"No," says the bear.

"NO, I don't want a bath.
NO, I hate being brushed.
NO, I won't go to bed . . ."

NO! NO! NO!"

Until Pearl calls out . . .

"STOP!"

"What about all this mess?" says Pearl.

"MESS?" says the bear.

"I don't know!

I've got to go!

GOODBYE!"

Out goes the bear.
And –

oh NO!

In comes *Mum!*

"What about all this mess?" says Mum.

And Pearl says,
"I will help tidy up.
I will wash my face.
I will brush my hair . . ."

And Pearl has
all she really wants –

1 lovely Mum,
1 huge hug
and 1 big kiss.